MW00890191

THE TURKEY TRAIN

By Steve Metzger

Illustrated by Jim Paillot

Cartwheel Books
An Imprint of Scholastic Inc.

TO MY LOVELY WIFE, LISA
—J.P.

TO KREBS
—S.M.

Text copyright © 2012 by Steve Metzger
Illustrations copyright © 2012 by Jim Paillot

All rights reserved. Published by Scholastic Inc. SCHOLASTIC, CARTWHEEL BOOKS,
and associated logos are trademarks and/or registered trademarks of Scholastic Inc.

No part of this publication may be reproduced, stored in a retrieval system,
or transmitted in any form or by any means, electronic, mechanical, photocopying,
recording, or otherwise, without written permission of the publisher.
For information regarding permission, write to Scholastic Inc.,
Attention: Permissions Department, 557 Broadway, New York, NY 10012.

ISBN 978-0-545-49229-4

10 9 8 7 6 5   16 17

Printed in the U.S.A. 40
First edition, November 2012

The display type was set in Sign Painter House Brush
The text was set in Contemporary Brush Bold
The art was created using Adobe Illustrator
Book design by Victor Joseph Ochoa

Wake up, Betty, Bill, and Jane!
Get ready for the Turkey Train!

Buy your tickets in Fort Wayne.
All aboard the Turkey Train!

Feathers ruffled? Don't complain.
Find your seat on the Turkey Train!

By afternoon we'll be in Maine.
Off we go on the Turkey Train!

Games and puzzles for your brain.

Make new friends on the Turkey Train!

Outside the window, pouring rain.
Warm and snug on the Turkey Train!

Rock and rollers entertain.
Sing and dance on the Turkey Train!

Stopping now near Lake Champlain.
Don't be late for the Turkey Train!

Over mountains, through the plain—
lots to see on the Turkey Train!

The engineer applied the brakes.
The Turkey Train slowed down.

From her window, Betty said,
"We're here! I see the town!"

The Turkey Train stopped at last.
The doors all opened wide.
Turkeys large and turkeys small
quickly raced outside.

Turkeys skating! Turkeys skiing!
Sledding down a hill!
Turkeys having snowball fights—
oops . . . one just hit Bill!

The turkeys played all afternoon,
until the sky grew black.
"We've had so much fun," said Jane,
"but now we must go back."

The turkeys were all in their seats.
No one could complain,
'cause everyone was fast asleep
on the Turkey Train.